Explore the extra

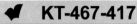

ROALD DAHL

You'll meet some **clever** tricksters here!

Mean MR and
MRS TWIT catch birds
to make pies and keep monkeys
in a cage in their garden.
They are **always** ready to play
horrible pranks on each other.

And read about how
MATILDA'S silly father finds
himself in a very **sticky** situation.

Bring Roald Dahl's extraordinary stories to life with the
Happy Studio app. Simply download the
app to a phone or tablet and read the
stories in this book aloud to
experience the fun.

The Glass Eye
and Bird Pie
from

THE TWITS

Mr Twit was one of those very hairy-faced men. The whole of his face except for his forehead, his eyes and his nose was covered with thick hair. The stuff even sprouted in revolting tufts out of his nostrils and ear-holes.

Mr Twit felt that this hairiness made him look terrifically wise and grand. But in truth he was neither of these things. Mr Twit was a twit. He was born a twit. And now at the age of sixty, he was a bigger twit than ever.

The hair on Mr Twit's face didn't grow smooth and matted as it does on most hairy-faced men. It grew in spikes that stuck out straight like the bristles of a nailbrush.

And how often did Mr Twit wash this bristly nailbrushy face of his?

The answer is NEVER, not even on Sundays.

He hadn't washed it for years.

Mrs Twit was no better than her husband.

She did not, of course, have a hairy face. It was a pity she didn't because that at any rate would have hidden some of her fearful ugliness.

Take a look at her. Have you ever seen a woman with an uglier face than that?

I doubt it.

But the funny thing is that Mrs Twit wasn't born ugly.

She'd had quite a nice face when she was young. The ugliness had grown upon her year by year as she got older.

Why would that happen?
I'll tell you why.
If a person has ugly
thoughts, it begins
to show on the
face.

And when
that person
has ugly thoughts
every day,
every week,
every year,

the face gets uglier and uglier until it gets so ugly you can hardly bear to look at it.

A person who has good thoughts cannot ever be ugly. You can have a wonky nose and a crooked mouth and a double chin and stick-out teeth, but if you have good thoughts they will shine out of your face like
sunbeams and
you will
always
look
lovely.

Nothing shone out of Mrs Twit's face.

In her right hand she carried a walking-stick. She used to tell people that this was because she had warts growing on the sole of her left foot and walking was painful. But the real reason she carried a stick was so that she could hit things with it, things like dogs and cats and small children.

And then there was the glass eye. Mrs Twit had a glass eye that was always looking the other way. You

can play a lot of tricks with a glass eye
because you can take it out and pop it
back in again any time you like. You
can bet your life Mrs Twit knew all
the tricks.

One morning she took out her glass eye and dropped it into Mr Twit's mug of beer when he wasn't looking.

Mr Twit sat there drinking the beer slowly. The froth made a white ring on the hairs around his mouth. He wiped the white froth on to his sleeve and wiped his sleeve on his trousers.

'You're plotting something,' Mrs Twit said, keeping her back turned so he wouldn't see that she had taken out her glass eye. 'Whenever you go all quiet like that I know very well you're plotting something.'

Mrs Twit was right. Mr Twit was
plotting away like mad. He was trying

to think up a really nasty trick he could play on his wife that day.

'You'd better be careful,' Mrs Twit said, 'because when I see you starting to plot, I watch you like a wombat.'

'Oh, do shut up, you old hag,' Mr Twit said. He went on drinking his beer.

Suddenly, as Mr Twit tipped the last drop of beer down his throat, he caught sight of Mrs Twit's awful glass eye staring up at him from the bottom of the mug. It made him jump.

'I told you I was watching you,' cackled Mrs Twit. 'I've got eyes everywhere so you'd better be careful.'

Once a week, on Wednesdays,
the Twits had Bird Pie for supper.
Mr Twit caught the birds and Mrs
Twit cooked them.

Mr Twit was good at catching birds.
On the day before Bird Pie day, he
would put the ladder up against The

Big Dead Tree in his garden and climb into the branches with a bucket of glue and a paint-brush. The glue he used was something called HUGTIGHT and it was stickier than any other glue in the world. He would paint it along the tops of all the branches and then go away.

As the sun went down, birds would fly in from all around to roost for the night in The Big Dead Tree. They didn't know, poor things, that the branches were all smeared with horrible HUGTIGHT. The moment they landed on a branch, their feet stuck and that was that.

The next morning, which was Bird Pie day, Mr Twit would climb up the ladder again and grab all the wretched birds that were stuck to the tree.

It didn't matter what kind they were – song thrushes, blackbirds, sparrows, crows, little jenny wrens, robins, anything – they all went into the pot for Wednesday's Bird Pie supper.

Not far from The Big Dead Tree, there was a monkey cage. There were four monkeys in it. They belonged to Mr Twit.

On one Tuesday evening after Mr Twit had been up the ladder and smeared the tree with HUGTIGHT, four little boys crept into the garden to look at the monkeys. They didn't care about the thistles and stinging-nettles, not when there were monkeys to look at.

After a while, they got tired of looking at the monkeys, so they explored further into the garden and found the ladder leaning against The Big Dead Tree. They decided to climb up it just for fun.

There's nothing wrong with that.

The next morning, when Mr Twit went out to collect the birds, he found four miserable little boys sitting in the tree, stuck as tight as could be by the seats of their pants to the branches. There were no birds because the presence of the boys had scared them away.

Mr Twit was furious. 'As there are no birds for my pie tonight,' he shouted, 'then it'll have to be *boys* instead!' He started to climb the ladder. 'Boy Pie might be better than Bird Pie,' he went on, grinning horribly. 'More meat and not so many tiny little bones!'

Colour me in!

The boys were terrified. 'He's going to boil us!' cried one of them.

'He'll stew us alive!' wailed the second one.

'He'll cook us with carrots!' cried the third.

But the fourth little boy, who had more sense than the others, whispered, 'Listen, I've just had an idea. We are only stuck by *the seats of our pants*. So quick! Unbutton your pants and slip out of them and fall to the ground.'

Mr Twit had reached the top of the ladder and was just about to make a grab for the nearest boy when they all suddenly tumbled out of the tree

and ran for home with their naked
bottoms winking at the sun.

The Twits **love** playing tricks on each other – and now they've played a **trick** on you by jumbling up the list of words below.

With the help of the **pictures**, can you work out what the words are?

B
I P
I R
D E

E M
K
N O
S Y

R
A D
B E

Do you have the **Happy Studio** app downloaded? Launch it **now** for an **extra** activity!

glass eye   glue   bird pie   monkeys   beard

The Hat and the Superglue

from

MATILDA

Matilda's parents owned quite a nice house with three bedrooms upstairs, while on the ground floor there was a dining-room and a living-room and a kitchen. Her father was a dealer in second-hand cars and it seemed he did pretty well at it. 'Sawdust,' he would say proudly, 'is one of the great secrets of my success.

And it costs me nothing. I get it free from the sawmill.'

'What do you use it for?' Matilda asked him.

'Ha!' the father said. 'Wouldn't you like to know.'

'I don't see how sawdust can help you to sell second-hand cars, Daddy.'

'That's because you're an ignorant little twit,' the father said. His speech was never very delicate but Matilda was used to it. She also knew that he liked to boast and she would egg him on shamelessly.

'You must be very clever to find a use for something that costs nothing,' she said. 'I wish I could do it.'

'You couldn't,' the father said. 'You're too stupid. But I don't mind telling young Mike here about it seeing as he'll be joining me in the business one day.' Ignoring Matilda, he turned to his son and said, 'I'm always glad to buy a car when some fool has

been crashing the gears so badly
they're all worn out and rattle like
mad. I get it cheap. Then all I do is
mix a lot of sawdust with the oil in the
gear-box and it runs as sweet as a nut.'

'How long will it run like that
before it starts rattling again?'
Matilda asked him.

'Long enough for the buyer to get a
good distance away,' the father said,
grinning. 'About a hundred miles.'

'But that's dishonest, Daddy,'
Matilda said. 'It's cheating.'

'No one ever got rich being honest,' the father said. 'Customers are there to be diddled.'

Mr Wormwood was a small ratty-looking man whose front teeth stuck out underneath a thin ratty moustache. He liked to wear jackets with large brightly coloured checks and he sported ties that were usually yellow or pale green. The Wormwood family were in the

36

living-room eating their suppers on their knees in front of the telly. The suppers were TV dinners in floppy aluminium containers with separate compartments for the stewed meat, the boiled potatoes and the peas. Mrs Wormwood sat munching her meal with her eyes glued to the American soap-opera on the screen.

She was a large woman whose hair was dyed platinum blonde except where you could see the mousy-brown bits growing out from the roots. She wore heavy make-up and she had one of those unfortunate bulging figures where the flesh appears to be strapped in all around the body to prevent it from falling out.

'Mummy,' Matilda said, 'would you mind if I ate my supper in the dining-room so I could read my book?'

The father glanced up sharply. '*I*

would mind!' he snapped. 'This is
a family gathering and no one leaves
the table till it's over!'

'But we're not at the table,' Matilda
said. 'We never are. We're always eating
off our knees and watching the telly.'

h watching the
: father said. His
become soft and

'Supper is
e leaves

ust herself to
answer him, so she kept quiet. She
could feel the anger boiling up
inside her. She knew it was wrong
to hate her parents like this, but she
was finding it very hard
not to do so. All the
reading she had done
had given her

a view of life that they had never
seen. If only they would read a little
they would soon discover there was
more to life than cheating people
and watching
television.

Another thing. She resented being told constantly that she was ignorant and stupid when she knew she wasn't. The anger inside her went on boiling and boiling, and as she lay in bed that night she made a decision. She decided that every time her father or her mother was beastly to her, she would get her own back in some way or another. A small victory or two would help her to tolerate their idiocies and would stop her from going crazy. You must remember that she was still hardly five years old and

it is not easy for somebody as small as that to score points against an all-powerful grown-up. Even

so, she was determined
to have a go. Her father,
after what had happened
in front of the telly that
evening, was first on
her list.

The following
morning, just before
the father left
for his beastly
second-hand
car garage,
Matilda

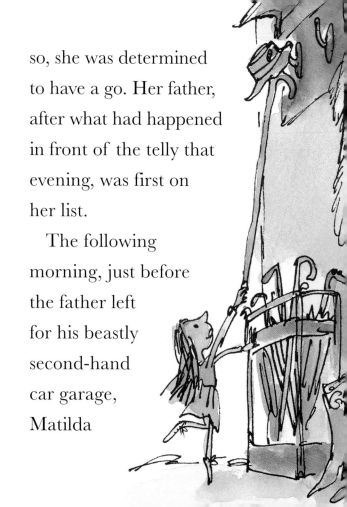

slipped into the cloakroom and got hold of the hat he wore each day to work. She had to stand on her toes and reach up as high as she could with a walking-stick in order to hook the hat off the peg, and even then she only just made it. The hat itself was one of those flat-topped pork-pie jobs with a jay's feather stuck in the hat-band and Mr Wormwood was very proud of it. He thought it gave him a rakish daring look,

45

especially when he wore it at an angle with his loud checked jacket and green tie.

Matilda, holding the hat in one hand and a thin tube of Superglue in the other, proceeded to squeeze a line of glue very neatly all round the inside rim of the hat. Then she carefully hooked the hat back on to the peg with the walking-stick. She timed this operation very carefully, applying the glue just as her father was getting up from the breakfast table.

Mr Wormwood didn't notice anything when he put the hat on, but when he arrived at the garage he couldn't get it off. Superglue is very powerful stuff, so powerful it will take your skin off if you pull too hard. Mr Wormwood didn't want to be scalped so he had to keep the hat on his head the whole day long, even when putting sawdust in gear-boxes and fiddling the mileages of cars with his electric drill. In an effort to save face, he adopted a casual attitude hoping that his staff would think that he actually *meant* to keep his hat on all day long just for the heck of it, like gangsters do in the films.

When he got home that evening he still couldn't get the hat off.

'Don't be silly,' his wife said. 'Come here. I'll take it off for you.'

She gave the hat a sharp yank. Mr Wormwood let out a yell that rattled the window-panes.

'Ow-w-w!' he screamed. 'Don't do that! Let go! You'll take half the skin off my forehead!'

Matilda, nestling in her usual chair, was watching this performance over the rim of her book with some interest.

'What's the matter, Daddy?' she said. 'Has your head suddenly swollen or something?'

The father glared at his daughter with deep suspicion, but said nothing. How could he? Mrs Wormwood said to him, 'It *must* be Superglue. It couldn't be anything else. That'll teach you to go playing round with nasty stuff like that. I expect you were trying to stick another feather in your hat.'

'I haven't touched the flaming

stuff!' Mr Wormwood shouted. He turned and looked again at Matilda, who looked back at him with large innocent brown eyes.

Mrs Wormwood said to him, 'You should read the label on the tube before you start messing with dangerous products. Always follow the instructions on the label.'

'What in heaven's name are you talking about, you stupid witch?' Mr Wormwood shouted, clutching the brim of his hat to stop anyone trying to pull it off again. 'D'you think I'm so stupid I'd glue this thing to my head on purpose?'

Matilda said, 'There's a boy down the road who got some Superglue on his finger without knowing it and then he put his finger to his nose.'

Mr Wormwood jumped. 'What happened to him?' he spluttered.

'The finger got stuck inside his nose,' Matilda said, 'and he had to go around like that for a week. People kept saying to him, "Stop picking your nose," and he couldn't do anything about it. He looked an awful fool.'

'Serve him right,' Mrs Wormwood said. 'He shouldn't have put his finger up there in the first place. It's a nasty habit. If all children had Superglue put on their fingers they'd soon stop doing it.'

Matilda said, 'Grown-ups do it too, Mummy. I saw you doing it yesterday in the kitchen.'

'That's quite enough from you,'

Mrs Wormwood said, turning pink.

Mr Wormwood had to keep his hat on all through supper in front of the television. He looked ridiculous and he stayed very silent.

When he went up to bed he tried again to get the thing off, and so did his wife, but it wouldn't budge. 'How am I going to have my shower?' he demanded.

'You'll just have to do without it, won't you,' his wife told him. And later on, as she watched her skinny little husband skulking around the bedroom in his purple-striped pyjamas with a pork-pie hat on his head, she thought how stupid he looked.

Hardly the kind of man a wife dreams about, she told herself.

Mr Wormwood discovered that the worst thing about having a permanent hat on his head was having to sleep in it. It was impossible to lie comfortably on the pillow. 'Now do stop fussing around,' his wife said to him after he had been tossing and turning for about an hour. 'I expect it will be loose by the morning and then it'll slip off easily.'

But it wasn't loose by the morning and it wouldn't slip off. So Mrs Wormwood took a pair of scissors and cut the thing off his head, bit by bit, first the top and then the brim.

Where the inner band had stuck to the hair all around the sides and back, she had to chop the hair off right to the skin so that he finished up with a bald white ring round his head, like some sort of a monk. And in the front, where the band had stuck directly to the bare skin, there remained a whole lot of small patches of brown leathery stuff that no amount of washing would get off.

At breakfast Matilda said to him, 'You *must* try to get those bits off your forehead, Daddy. It looks as though you've got little brown insects crawling about all over you. People will think you've got lice.'

'Be quiet!' the father snapped. 'Just keep your nasty mouth shut, will you!'

All in all it was a most satisfactory exercise.

When Matilda **tricks** her father
into getting his hat **stuck** on
his head, he is **desperate**
to remove it.

Could you
invent a better contraption
to remove it, instead of Mrs Wormwood
having to cut it off with scissors?